$ 8.08

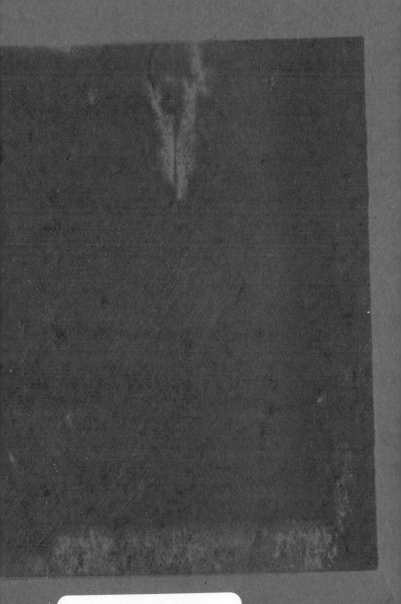

Yellow Butter Purple Jelly Red Jam Black Bread

Yellow Butter
Purple Jelly
Red Jam
Black Bread

Poems by **MARY ANN HOBERMAN**

Illustrated by **CHAYA BURSTEIN**

The Viking Press
New York

In memory of my father,
who loved to play

First Edition
Text Copyright © 1981 by Mary Ann Hoberman
Illustrations Copyright © 1981 by Chaya Burstein
All rights reserved
First published in 1981 by The Viking Press
625 Madison Avenue, New York, New York   10022
Published simultaneously in Canada by Penguin Books Canada Limited
Printed in U.S.A.
1   2   3   4   5   85   84   83   82   81

Library of Congress Cataloging in Publication Data
Hoberman, Mary Ann
Yellow butter, purple jelly, red jam, black bread.
Summary: Includes 58 poems on a variety of subjects.
1. Children's poetry, American.   [1. American
poetry]   I. Burstein, Chaya.   II. Title.
PS3558.03367Y35   813'.54   80-26555
ISBN 0-670-79382-5

YELLOW BUTTER

Yellow butter purple jelly red jam black bread

Spread it thick
Say it quick

Yellow butter purple jelly red jam black bread

Spread it thicker
Say it quicker

Yellow butter purple jelly red jam black bread

Now repeat it
While you eat it

Yellow butter purple jelly red jam black bread

Don't talk
With your mouth full!

QUESTION

The grownups say I'm growing tall
And that my clothes are growing small.
Can clothes grow *small*?
I always think
That things grow *big*
Or else they shrink.
But did they shrink
Or did I grow
Or did we both change?
I don't know.

COMPARISON

John is the tallest—he's ever so high;
Betty's a little bit taller than I;
I'm not as tall as Betty is tall;
But John is the tallest, the tallest of all.
 Tall, taller, tallest,
 One, two, and three.
 Both John and Betty
 Stretch high over me.
But turn it around and it's better for me
Because I'm the shortest of all the three.
 Short, shorter, shortest,
 Hello and good-bye.
 I am the shortest;
 The shortest am I.

Betty's the oldest—six last July;
John isn't six but he's older than I;
I'm not as old since I'm just over four;
John's a bit older and Betty's much more.
 Old, older, oldest,
 One, two, and three.
 Both John and Betty
 Are years beyond me.
But turn it around and it's better for me
Because I'm the youngest of all the three.
 Young, younger, youngest,
 Hello and good-bye.
 I am the youngest;
 The youngest am I.

WHEN I WAS YOUNG AND FOOLISH

When I was young and foolish
And wished that I were fair
I wore a wig upon my head
To hide my horrid hair.

But when I looked into my glass
I loathed the look of that
And so I hid my horrid wig
Beneath a handsome hat.

I looked into my mirror
I smiled a little smile
But though I pushed and pulled the hat
It still was not my style.

I covered it with feathers
I covered it with lace
I looked into my mirror
And made a little face.

I bought a pretty bonnet
I put it on the stack
I looked into the mirror
My face made faces back.

I decked the pile with flowers
Till it was twice my size
But still the look was not quite right
At least above the eyes.

The years went by
The rains came down
The winds began to blow
The hats were toppled off my head
My face felt very low.

My nose grew long and narrow
My eyes grew very big
The hairs began to dance and sing
And wiggled off the wig.

My ears began to wriggle
My whiskers swayed and shook
I'll never wear a wig again
No matter how I look.

BIRTHDAYS

If birthdays happened once a week
Instead of once a year,
Think of all the gifts you'd get
And all the songs you'd hear
And think how quickly you'd grow up;
Wouldn't it feel queer
If birthdays happened once a week
Instead of once a year?

TIME

Listen to the clock strike
One
    two
        three,
Up in the tall tower
One
    two
        three.
Hear the hours slowly chime;
Watch the hands descend and climb;
Listen to the sound of time
One
    two
        three.

CHANGING

I know what *I* feel like;
I'd like to be *you*
And feel what *you* feel like
And do what *you* do.
I'd like to change places
For maybe a week
And look like your look-like
And speak as you speak
And think what you're thinking
And go where you go
And feel what you're feeling
And know what you know.
I wish we could do it;
What fun it would be
If I could try you out
And you could try me.

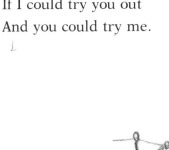

ANTHROPOIDS

The next time you go to the zoo
The zoo
Slow down for a minute or two
Or two
      And consider the apes,
      All their sizes and shapes,
For they all are related to you
To you.

Yes, they all are related to you
To you
And they all are related to me
To me
      To our fathers and mothers,
      Our sisters and brothers
And all of the people we see
We see.

8

The chimpanzees, gorillas, and all
And all
The orangutans climbing the wall
The wall
    These remarkable creatures
    Share most of our features
And the difference between us is small
Quite small.

So the next time you go to the zoo
The zoo
Slow down for a minute or two
Or two
    And consider the apes,
    All their sizes and shapes,
For they all are related to you
To you.

TAPIR

The tapir has a tubby torse.
He is not very big.
Although related to the horse,
He looks more like a pig.

If I were in the tapir's shoes
(Although I'm not, of course),
Relation to the pig I'd choose,
Resemblance to the horse.

A THOUGHT

   Think of a whale.
Then
   Think of a snail.
Then
   Think of a snail on the tail of a whale.
Then
   Think of the tail of the whale with no snail.

A whale is so big
And a snail is so small
That there's hardly a difference at all
   between
The snail on the tail
And the tail
With no snail.

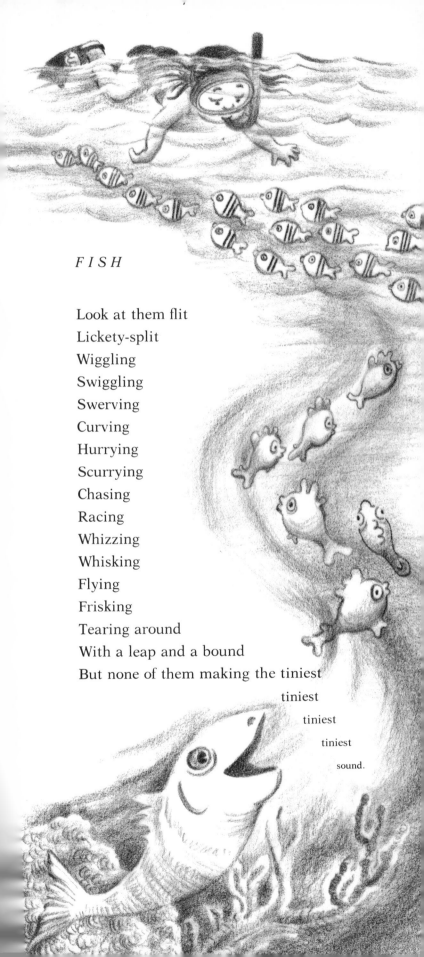

FISH

Look at them flit
Lickety-split
Wiggling
Swiggling
Swerving
Curving
Hurrying
Scurrying
Chasing
Racing
Whizzing
Whisking
Flying
Frisking
Tearing around
With a leap and a bound
But none of them making the tiniest
tiniest
tiniest
tiniest
sound.

WISH

I'd like to be
A kangaroo
And have a pocket
Made of me.

THE LLAMA WHO HAD NO PAJAMA

The llama who had no pajama
Was troubled and terribly sad
When it became known that he had outgrown
Every pair of pajamas he had;
And he tearfully said to his mama
In a voice that was deep with despair:
O llamaly mama
I need a pajama
Or what in the world will I wear?
Or what in the world,
In the wumberly world,
In the wumberly world will I wear?

The llama who had no pajama
Looked up at the evening sky.
It will soon, he said, be time for bed
And all will be sleeping but I.
And all will be sleeping but I, but I,
And all will be sleeping but I.

For how can a llama go bare to bed,
The little pajamaless llama said,
When the rest of the world,
Of the wumberly world,
Are all wearing pretty pajamas?

The poor little llama's sad mama
Got out her needle and thread.
I'll try to enlarge your pajama,
The llama's sad mama said.
And she stitched and she sewed those pajamas
Till she ran out of plum-colored thread
But they still were too small for the llama.
O what will we do? mama said.
For you must have a pair of pajamas
As you cannot go naked to bed;
But where in the world,
In the wumberly world,
Will we find you a pair of pajamas?

They looked in each nook and each cranny;
They looked on each hillock and mound;
But though they saw bathrobes and bonnets,
Pajamas were not to be found.
The clock struck a quarter to seven,
The llama lay down on the ground.
I know I won't sleep, he sniffed sadly
And his nose made a staying-up sound.

But he did sleep. He dozed off at seven
And he slept for the rest of the night
And when he woke up in the morning
To his mama he said with delight:

What a wonderful sleep I've been sleeping all
    night!
My head feels so clear and my eyes feel so
    bright.
When we looked for pajamas, how foolish we
    were.
Why, I sleep so much better in nothing but fur!
It fits me so nicely; it's light as the air;
It's the practical thing for a llama to wear.
And since goats don't wear coats
And doves don't wear gloves
And cocks don't wear socks
And bats don't wear hats,
Well, why in the world,
In the wumberly world,
Should llamas be wearing pajamas?

THE FOLK WHO LIVE IN BACKWARD TOWN

The folk who live in Backward Town
Are inside out and upside down.
They wear their hats inside their heads
And go to sleep beneath their beds.
They only eat the apple peeling
And take their walks across the ceiling.

WHENEVER

Whenever I want my room to move,
I give myself a twirl
And busily, dizzily whiz about
In a reeling, wheeling whirl.
Then I spin in a circle as fast as I can
Till my head is weak from churning
Like a tipsy top. . . .
And then I stop.
    But my room goes right on turning.

THE TEAPOT AND THE KETTLE

Said the teapot to the kettle,
"You are really in fine fettle,
You're a handsome piece of metal
Are you not, not, not?

"Your dimensions are so spacious,
And your waistline so capacious
And your whistle so flirtatious
When your water's hot."

Said the kettle, "Why, you flatter
Me extremely, but no matter,
I have never seen a fatter
Teapot in my life.

"Though I would not call you dumpy,
You are round and sweet and plumpy
And I'm sure you're never grumpy.
Would you be my wife?"

Said the teapot to the kettle,
"Sir, my given name is Gretel
And I'd really like to settle
Down your wife to be."

So without the least delay
They were married the next day
And they both were very gay
Drinking tea, tea, tea.

EXCURSION

I put my honey in her pram.
I pushed my honey to the store.
I bought my honey a stick of candy.
Honey said, Now ain't that dandy?
Storeman said, I want some money.
Honey said, Now ain't that funny?
Money for a stick of candy!
Do you have some money handy?
I paid the man a silver dime.
(Had it with me all the time.)
I put my honey in her pram.
I pushed her home
And here I am.

OAK LEAF PLATE

Oak leaf plate
Acorn cup
Raindrop tea
Drink it up!

Sand for salt
Mud for pie
Twiggy chops
Fine to fry.

Sticks for bread
Stones for meat
Grass for greens
Time to eat!

RABBIT

A rabbit
bit
A little bit
An itty bitty
Little bit of beet.
Then bit
By bit
He bit
Because he liked the taste of it.
But when he bit
A wee bit more,
It was more bitter than before.
"This beet is bitter!"
Rabbit cried.
"I feel a bit unwell inside!"
But when he bit
Another bite, that bit of beet
Seemed quite all right.
Besides
hen all is said and done,
Better bitter beet
than none.

MEG'S EGG

Meg
Likes
A *reg*ular egg
Not a poached
Or a fried
But a *reg*ular egg
Not a deviled
Or coddled
Or scrambled
Or boiled
But an *egg*ular
*Meg*ular
*Reg*ular
Egg!

A CATCH

I've caught a fish!
Come look!
I've got him on my hook.
He saw my worm down in the pond
And fishes all are very fond
Of worms, so up he swam to mine
And now I've got him on my line.
He's just the proper size to munch.
(I think I'll have him fried for lunch.)

WAITERS

Dining with his older daughter
Dad forgot to order water.
Daughter quickly called the waiter.
Waiter said he'd bring it later.
So she waited, did the daughter,
Till the waiter brought her water.
When he poured it for her later,
Which one would you call the waiter?

APPLESAUCE

Shall I dig a hole?
Shall I make it deep?
Shall I slope the sides?
Shall I make them steep?
Shall I scoop a path?
Shall I make it wide?
Shall I pile a mountain
       Over on the side?
Shall I point the top?
Shall I push the tip?
Shall I let it slide?
Shall I let it slip?
Shall I let it hide
       The path across the plate?
Shall I curve the path?
Shall I make it straight?
Shall I fill it up?
Shall I smooth it flat?
Shall I draw a dog?
Shall I draw a cat?
Shall I build a house?
Shall I make a street?
Shall I dig a hole?
       Or
Shall I start to eat?

LET'S DRESS UP

Let's dress up in grown-up clothes:
       Swishing skirts
       That touch our toes;
       Wispy veils
       That hide our nose.
Let's dress up today.

       Feathered bonnet
       Trimmed with lace;
       Rouge and lipstick
       On our face;
       An umbrella
       (Just in case).
Let's dress up today.

Now we're ready.
Let's go walking
Down the street
(Pretend we're talking).
       Walking
       Talking
       Walking
       Talking,
All dressed up today.

YOU'RE MRS. COBBLE AND I'M MRS. FROME

You're Mrs. Cobble and I'm Mrs. Frome.
"Hello, Mrs. Cobble. How nice you could come.
And how are you feeling?"
    "Oh, down in the dumps.
    Six of the children are sick with the
    mumps."
"Good heavens, my dear!
(We have chickenpox here.)"
    "Isn't it awful?"
"Isn't it grim?"
    "And how is your husband?"
"Don't ask about *him!*
He's down with a fever. One hundred and nine."
    "One hundred and *nine!* Did you hear about
    mine?
    He fell from a ladder but now he is fine."
"Isn't it dreadful?"
    "Isn't it sad?"
"A bee stung the baby."
    "Oh, that was too bad."
"But now she's recovered."
    "Oh, is she? I'm glad."
"Well, I must be going. Come visit me soon."
    "Why, thank you, I'd like to some nice
    afternoon."
"Good-bye, Mrs. Cobble."
    "Good-bye, Mrs. Frome."
And you walk out the door and high-heel your
    way home.

HERE WE GO

Here we go
To and fro
Pushing our carriages nice and slow
Up and down
Through the town
Taking a walk with our babies.

Tuck them in
Toe to chin
Shawls fastened tight with a safety pin
Back and forth
South and north
Taking a walk with our babies.

Off they glide
On their ride
Snug in their carriages side by side
Rain or shine
It's so fine
Taking a walk with our babies.

TIMOTHY TOPPIN

Timothy Toppin climbed up a tree
    He would not come down
He climbed to the tippety top of the tree
    He would not come down
His father and mother were begging him please
His sister and brother were down on their knees
"Timothy, Timothy, don't be a tease."
    But he absolutely would not come down.

Timothy Toppin climbed up a tree
    He would not come down
He climbed to the tippety top of the tree
    He would not come down
"I can touch the sky if I try," said he.
"There isn't a thing that I can't see,
And what's even better, you can't see me
    So why should I ever come down?"

Timothy Toppin stayed seventy years
    He would not come down
His mother and father were close to tears
    He would not come down
And then when he was seventy-four
He climbed down the trunk and he walked in
    the door
And he said, "I don't want to stay up any more
    And that's why I finally came down."

BROTHER

I had a little brother
And I brought him to my mother
And I said I want another
Little brother for a change.

But she said don't be a bother
So I took him to my father
And I said this little bother
Of a brother's very strange.

But he said one little brother
Is exactly like another
And every little brother
Misbehaves a bit, he said.

So I took the little bother
From my mother and my father
And I put the little bother
Of a brother back to bed.

IT'S DARK OUT

It's dark out
It's dark out
Although the hour's early;
It isn't even five o'clock
And yet it's dark all down the block
Because the season's winter
And the sun has gone to bed.

SNOW

Snow
Snow
Lots of snow
Everywhere we look and everywhere we go
Snow in the sandbox
Snow on the slide
Snow on the bicycle
Left outside
Snow on the steps
And snow on my feet
Snow on the sidewalk
Snow on the sidewalk
Snow on the sidewalk
Down the street.

A YEAR LATER

Last summer I couldn't swim at all;
I couldn't even float;
I had to use a rubber tube
Or hang on to a boat;
I had to sit on shore
While everybody swam;
But now it's this summer
And I can!

WAGER

If I
Were dry
And you
Were, too,
And it
Began
To rain
A bit,
And home
You got
But I
Did not,
I bet
I'd get
More wet
Than you.

INDIAN PIPE

Blueberries
Blueberries
Blueberries ripe!
And I just found a clump of Indian pipe
Slender and white at the foot of an oak
Where perhaps long ago a whisper of smoke
Twisted up through the air
And out over this land
As an Indian stood
With his pipe in his hand
Right here in this wood
Right here where I stand.

BUTTERFISH BAY

I rowed the boat over to Butterfish Bay
(Butterfish Bay is quite far away).
I took my lunch in a paper sack
And said that I didn't know when I'd be back:
I might get caught in a terrible squall
And then I'd never get back at all,
Or the boat might tip over and I might drown,
Or I might spend the night in Butterfish Town;
All kinds of things happen to ships at sea.
That's all very well, said Mother to me,
As long as you're home at half past three.

WAY DOWN DEEP

Underneath the water
Way down deep
In sand and stones and seaweed
Starfish creep
Snails inch slowly
Oysters sleep
Underneath the water
Way down deep.

F R O G

Pollywiggle
Pollywog
Tadpole
Bullfrog
Leaps on
Long legs
Jug-o-rum
Jelly eggs
Sticky tongue
Tricks flies
Spied by
Flicker eyes
Wet skin
Cold blood
Squats in
Mucky mud
Leaps on
Long legs
Jug-o-rum
Jelly eggs
Laid in
Wet bog. . . .
Pollywiggle
Pollywog.

WHALE

A whale is stout about the middle,
He is stout about the ends,
& so is all his family
& so are all his friends.

He's pleased that he's enormous,
He's happy he weighs tons,
& so are all his daughters
& so are all his sons.

He eats when he is hungry
Each kind of food he wants,
& so do all his uncles
& so do all his aunts.

He doesn't mind his blubber,
He doesn't mind his creases,
& neither do his nephews
& neither do his nieces.

You may find him chubby,
You may find him fat,
But he would disagree with you:
He likes himself like that.

FAMILY FRIENDS

Mrs. Goose had a family of gay little geese;
Mrs. Moose had a family of meek little meese;
And they lived on the river
Not far from the bay,
Borrowed sugar and cream
In a neighborly way;
All the mooses were brown;
All the gooses were gray;
And they played very nicely together.

The mooses were big and the gooses were small
But that didn't seem much to matter at all;
The gooses took rides on the mooses' broad
    backs
And they all played at leapfrog and lotto and
    jacks
And when they were hungry
They went home for snacks,
And they played very nicely together.

Each morning at daybreak before the sun rose
They sat by the river and dangled their toes
And each evening at sundown before the night
     comes
They sat by the river and twiddled their thumbs
Sipping pink lemonade,
Munching big purple plums,
Playing ever so nicely together.

When the weather is clear and the forest is still,
If you climb to the rock at the top of the hill
And look down on the river, not far from the
     bay,
You can still see the mooses and gooses at play.
At least I've been told.
At least so they say.
They are still playing nicely together.

HOW MANY?

A mother skunk all black and white
Leads her babies down the street
       Pitter patter
       Pitter patter
       Pitter patter
       TWENTY feet.

Off they toddle slow and steady
Making tiny twitter cries
       Flitter flutter
       Flitter flutter
       Flitter flutter
       TEN small eyes.

Nose to tail-tip in procession
Single-file the family trails
       Flippy floppy
       Flippy floppy
       Flippy floppy
       FIVE long tails.

Up the street a dog comes barking,
Sees the strangers, leaps pell-mell . . .
    Ickle pickle
    Ickle pickle
    Ickle pickle
    ONE BIG SMELL!

HIPPOPOTAMUS

How far from human beauty
Is the hairless hippopotamus
With such a square enormous head
And such a heavy botamus.

OCELOT

The ocelot's a clever cat.
She knowsalot of this and that.
She growsalot of spotted fur
Which looks extremely well on her.

In places where it snowsalot
She seldom ever goesalot.
She much prefers it where it's hot.
That's all about the ocelot.

CAMEL

The camel has a heavy bump

upon his back.

It's called a hump.

Although it weighs him down, he moves

with perfect grace

upon his hooves.

GIRAFFES

I like them.
Ask me why.
    Because they hold their heads so high.
    Because their necks stretch to the sky.
    Because they're quiet, calm, and shy.
    Because they run so fast they fly.
    Because their eyes are velvet brown.
    Because their coats are spotted tan.
    Because they eat the tops of trees.
    Because their legs have knobby knees.
    Because
    Because
    Because. That's why
I like giraffes.

GAZELLE

O gaze on the graceful gazelle as it grazes
It grazes on green growing leaves and on grasses
On grasses it grazes, go gaze as it passes
It passes so gracefully, gently, O gaze!

I'D LIKE TO

I'd like to dress in satin
I'd like to dress in silk
I'd like to have a nanny goat
To give me nanny milk.

I'd like to dress in flannel
I'd like to dress in fur
I'd like to have a pussycat
And listen to her purr.

TIGER

I'm a tiger
Striped with fur
Don't come near
Or I might Grrr
Don't come near
Or I might growl
Don't come near
Or I might
BITE!

ADVICE

If you're sleepy in the jungle
And you wish to find a pillow,
Take a friendly word of warning:
DO NOT USE AN ARMADILLO!

Though an armadillo often
May roll up just like a pillow,
Do not go by his appearance
But go by with ample clearance.

For an armadillo's armor
Is not suited for a pillow,
And an armadillo's temper
Only suits an armadillo.

If you use him for a pillow,
Then beware of what will follow:
He may slip out while you're sleeping
And an arm or two he'll swallow.

(And any beast that leaves you armless
Can't be classified as harmless!)

Nor will he beg your pardon
For his thoughtless peccadillo;
So the next time you go walking in the jungle
TAKE A PILLOW!

PENGUIN

O Penguin, do you ever try
To flap your flipper wings and fly?
How do you feel, a bird by birth
And yet for life tied down to earth?
A feathered creature, born with wings
Yet never wingborne. All your kings
And emperors must wonder why
Their realm is sea instead of sky.

LOOK

Look
Look
Out in the grass
A bumblebee on some sassafras!
Look
Look
Up in the tree
A big black crow and a chickadee!
Look again
On the garden path
A bug in a puddle taking a bath!

ANTS

I like to watch the ants at work
When I am out at play.
I like to see them run about
And carry crumbs away.

And when I plug an anthill door
To keep them in their den,
I like to see them find a way
To get outside again.

THERE ONCE WAS A PIG

There once was a pig
And she wore a wig
With golden ringlets hanging down
And all the pigs
Said, "Piggy wig,
You're the prettiest pig in Parkertown.
      The perkiest pig
      The porkiest pig
      The pinkiest pig in Parkertown."

And all the hogs
Waddled out of their bogs
To see this pig of great renown
Saying, "Sister Sow,
We do allow
You're the prettiest pig in Parkertown.
      The plumpiest pig
      The pluckiest pig
      The pinkiest pig in Parkertown."

Then all the pigs
Put on big wigs
With golden ringlets hanging down
And danced jig jogs
With all the hogs
They danced all over Parkertown.
      Danced jiggety jigs
      Danced joggety jogs
      The pigs and the hogs of Parkertown.

HOW FAR

How far
How far
How far is today
When tomorrow has come
And it's yesterday?

Far
And far
And far away.

SLOTH

A tree's a trapeze for a sloth.
He clings with his claws to its growth.
    Both the sloth and his wife
    Lead an upside-down life.
To lead such a life I'd be loath.

BRACHIOSAURUS

This dinosaur is now extinct
While I am still extant.
I'd like to bring it back alive.
        (Unhappily I can't.)
The largest ones weighed fifty tons
And stood three stories high.
Their dinner ration? Vegetation.
        (Never hurt a fly.)
Alas! Alack! They're dead and gone
Through failure to adapt
And only known by track and bone.
        (I wish we'd overlapped.)

THE KING OF UMPALAZZO

O the King of Umpalazzo
Is very big and fat;
He eats raw steak and chocolate cake
And grouse and mouse and rat,
And veal and eel and Hudson seal
And cracker meal and lemon peel
And dogs that bark and pigs that squeal;
What *do* you think of that?

O the King of Umpalazzo
Is very, very old;
His beard is long and yellow;
His feet are always cold.
His face is full of wrinkles;
His eyesight is quite dim;
He's a silly old billy
Who's always too chilly;
What *do* you think of him?

O the King of Umpalazzo
Is very, very nice;
He says, "I thank you," once a day
And he says, "You're welcome," twice.
He nods his head and tips his hat
And shakes your hand and walks his cat.
He never tells you not to speak
And he gives out ice cream every week.
He's a funny old honey,
As soft as a bunny;
What *do* you think
    What *do* you think
        What *do* you think of that?

THE BIRTHDAY BUS

My birthday is coming and I will be six;
I'd like a new bike and some peppermint sticks;
But if someone decided to give me a bus,
I'd accept it at once without making a fuss.

I'd tell all of my friends to come quickly inside
And I'd take them all out for a wonderful ride.
If somebody wanted to stop, they'd just buzz
And I'd stop in a minute, wherever I was;
And if somebody had somewhere special to go,
I'd drive there at once and I'd never say no.

The ride would be free; they would each have a
      seat;
And every half hour I'd hand out a treat.
I'd pull up at a bus stop; I'd put on the brake
And I'd pass around ice cream and soda and
      cake.
Then when they were finished, I'd call out,
      "Hi-ho!
Hold on to your hats, everybody! Let's go!"
(But if anyone asked me to please let them drive,
I'd say driving is dangerous for children of five.)

My birthday is coming and I will be six;
I'd like a new bike and some peppermint sticks;
But if someone decided to give me a bus,
I'd accept it at once without making a fuss.

I WAS RIDING TO POUGHKEEPSIE

I was riding to Poughkeepsie
When I met a green-eyed gypsy,
A green-eyed Spanish gypsy
In a gold and scarlet gown.

And she told me she was roaming
From Poughkeepsie to Wyoming,
Through the West to wild Wyoming
Where the icy winds blow down.

Ride beside me through the mountains,
By the bubble-blowing fountains,
Said the green-eyed Spanish gypsy
In her gold and scarlet gown.

But I left the green-eyed gypsy
And continued to Poughkeepsie,
Up the highway to Poughkeepsie,
Up to plain Poughkeepsie town.

HELLO AND GOOD-BYE

Hello and good-bye
Hello and good-bye

When I'm in a swing
Swinging low and then high,
Good-bye to the ground
Hello to the sky.

Hello to the rain
Good-bye to the sun,
Then hello again sun
When the rain is all done.

In blows the winter,
Away the birds fly.
Good-bye and hello
Hello and good-bye.

INDEX OF FIRST LINES